BIKER'S STOLEN BABY

Dark Mafia MC Romance

Gabrielle Melo

ISBN: 9798840566596
Imprint: Independently published

1st edition

Cover design by: Gabrielle Melo

CONTENTS

CHAPTER 1

Barbara

I hated the life I was living. I didn't know what I was doing in this place. Was I thinking that my husband was suddenly going to change? Obviously not.

I was at his party, and yet I wasn't.

I was in the middle of the crowd and I was holding something in my hand. I was so out of it that I wasn't even thinking about what it was that I was holding in my hand.

Perhaps it was a glass. A glass of wine or something of the sort, but I really wasn't thinking about it. Just couldn't care less.

The only thing that I cared about was that the taste was good. Whenever my lips touched it, it felt good. It made me feel something that my husband couldn't anymore.

I really thought that marrying a biker was a good idea.

At the time, I thought that it was everything I wanted, but then I realized how shitty my life had become.

He was ruthless. The only thing he wanted was a baby, but I wasn't ready for it, and I certainly wasn't thinking about living with him for the rest of my life.

It wasn't that he didn't love me. I was certain that he did, but it wasn't going to change anything.

I just couldn't keep living this life where I had to be worried about my well-being and safety all the time.

The thing with the Punishers MC was that they were a part of the 1% and they had enemies going after them all the time, even after they promised themselves they were going to be better. *They didn't.* Even after the incident with Lazar and Gleb, we all thought that it would get better, but it didn't.

I took a deep breath, trying to recompose myself so that I didn't feel like I was in a dream anymore.

I was here. I was at this party and it was tolerable, despite the smelly environment and the even smellier people. I initially thought that I really liked big, hulky, and rough men, but it turned out that it was nothing more than something that used to get me off when I was feeling confused about myself.

But now that I was here at this party, having to listen to this terrible, eardrum-shattering music, the only thing I wanted was to have someone more romantic with his arm wrapped around my waist, and telling me that everything was going to be okay because he was going to take me home.

I looked down at my belly, wondering if I would ever have a baby.

The thing was that Pavel wanted one, but I couldn't make his wish come true. We'd tried sometimes already, but it didn't work.

And he was always so busy that we didn't have time to go to the doctor so that our problem could be elucidated. We really should do that. I was getting worried that I was infertile, or that he might be.

Either way, we would never find out the truth without first going to the doctor, and things were so bad around here that we didn't even have money for that.

I took a deep breath in and turned around slowly, finding, in the crowd, none other than his best friend.

Our eyes locked.

In a blink, I felt something different.

I already knew him well. Well, as well as I could. He was a little mysterious, even though he was kind of my only friend at the moment.

He was someone that I could rely on when things were going bad for me, just like now.

He was looking at me through the crowd, and I could almost read what he was thinking about.

He was worried about me, wasn't he?

He wanted to come to me right at this moment to ask me about what I was thinking and what was getting me so worried, but that wasn't so easy.

For one, his best friend and my husband was still at the party. He was chatting and bantering with his buddies, sure, but he was still over there and I was certain that he would find me with his eyes the moment that I was talking with Igor, something that could lead to further complications.

Still, I just couldn't stay here in the middle of this crowd, doing nothing and pretending that I was drinking from the wine glass I was holding in my hand.

It was surprising that I even had a wine glass in my hand, considering that this was a party for bikers and not for someone with standards a little higher, like me.

I never thought that my husband would even think that I preferred to be holding a wine glass in my hand instead of a beer can.

I took a deep breath and then I started to walk to one of the other rooms in the house where the party was taking place.

Even though the Punishers MC was a biker club, we didn't have a proper biker club building. Not anymore, anyway. Ever since the incident with Lazar and Gleb, things were like that.

My husband tried to explain to me why things were that way. He said that it was for the better. In case the police came for us, we would be able to get out and flee from them before it was too late, and before they could gather any more evidence against us than they already had.

I shared his sentiment and decision. The other bikers, though, didn't think the same way. We all thought that we had to establish our roots in the ground again and gift ourselves another biker club building.

For now, things were going to remain the way they were, though, and for me, it was better.

I took a deep breath in and I found myself in another room, and this one was much quieter than the other one where I was.

Did I have friends here at the party? Not at all. I had some friends once. *Had,* I should emphasize. The moment they found out I was getting married to Pavel was when they decided they didn't need me anymore.

Just thinking about them, I felt rage bubbling up in my veins. It wasn't that they thought I'd never been their friend, but that they didn't care about me enough to keep supporting me even through these difficult times.

I shook my head, deciding not to think about them at the moment. It was not worth it.

I turned around the moment that I found Igor coming in my direction. The moment that my eyes found his was the moment that I looked over my shoulder to make sure that my husband wasn't looking at me.

I was happy when I discovered that he couldn't, unless he came into this room, something that I was certain he wasn't going to do.

He was drunk. I knew that the moment that I had looked at him when he was still chatting with his friends. He was having so much fun, wasn't he? The way he laughed, smiled, joked, and pretty much everything else he did with them showed me as much.

I knew what my mother would be saying to me right now if she was here with me. She would be saying that I had to 'man up' and kick my husband out of my life. If only it were so easy.

The thing about him was that even though he said he loved me, I knew how dangerous it would be to get a divorce.

And it was precisely how much he loved me that I just couldn't get a divorce even though I wanted to so much.

I just feared for my whole family. He knew them so well.

"Party not up to your standards?" Igor asked, approaching me.

I always confided so much in him, but we never did anything together more than just talking, even though I found him to be extremely handsome.

I didn't like to be thinking about it this way, but there was just no denying it.

He was my type.

He was tall.

He was imposing, and his eyes always looked at me as though he could read everything I was thinking and tell me that everything was going to be fine.

But not everything was going to be fine. I had a husband whose life was always at risk, who wanted a baby, and who I was certain would not come back home tonight because of how drunk he was.

Just thinking about that, I couldn't help but feel my rage bubbling up in my veins.

"You know that it's not about that. I'm just thinking about my life. You know what has happened to my mother, and I keep worrying about her," I said, tightening my grip on the wine glass.

Ever since she hit her head and couldn't open her eyes anymore, I wondered what was going to happen to her. Would she ever wake up and defeat her coma?

My family was paying her hospital bills, but we weren't certain for how much longer we could keep doing that, and it was beginning to corrode everything that we were.

We weren't a great family, but the fact that my mother was still in the hospital, still on the hospital bed and only breathing thanks to some machines was really destroying the little we had.

And it was making me feel so much more desperate about everything going on.

I supposed that was the reason why I was feeling a little better with Igor around.

CHAPTER 2

Igor

I knew what she was going through. Knew it so well. After all, she always told me everything. She always told me about everything going on in her life, to the point where I felt I was pretty much the only person she could confide anything in.

Barbara was so stunning.

Ginger hair.

Green eyes.

A little on the curvy side, which for me was perfect.

The only thing I wanted right now was to grab her, put my hands on her waist, kiss her, and then tell her that everything was going to be fine.

After all, looking into her eyes, I could tell that she was on the verge of crying.

I had no idea what Pavel thought he was doing. So he was throwing this party, but was it really serving any purpose other than stroking his own ego, making other people think that the Punishers MC were still a force to be reckoned with?

Obviously not.

The more I thought about it, the more I was certain that he wasn't giving his wife enough attention.

I knew it was wrong, but doing the wrong thing was exciting and I could never change that.

There was some sexual tension between us, and I could see

it in her eyes, the way she was looking at me, the way that she moved her eyes up and down, checking every part of me.

There was a small table by my side and I was happy that it was there. It allowed me to set the wine glass down there. While everyone was getting piss drunk from their beer cans, I preferred the wine glass I had in my hand.

And another reason why I preferred it was because I knew that Barbara was going to like that, and looking into her eyes right now, I knew that she was.

What was I thinking I was doing? I asked myself, realizing that this was so wrong that it would hurt Pavel.

But that was the thing. After everything I had to have to keep witnessing him doing, I thought that he deserved it. Here I was with the most stunning woman in the world and I knew how much he was wasting.

Man just didn't know what he was losing, and that made me feel my rage bubbling in my veins.

"You know that my husband shouldn't see us together," she said, but her voice was weak.

It wasn't like what she was saying was going to stop me.

Maybe this was the opportunity I was looking for, or maybe this was just the alcohol affecting me.

After all, in the other times where I was with Barbara, I had never been so bold.

"I don't think that Pavel is even going to come here."

"That's bullshit. You know that he's always watching me, even when he thinks he isn't."

"You're paranoid about him and you. Your mother is in a coma and yet he's throwing parties like it's nothing. Do you think that's right?"

"You're his friend. Why are you saying these things? Do you think that I'm going to fall for you or something like that? It's never going to happen, and you know it."

I liked her fiery attitude and nothing she could ever say would ever change that about me.

"The fact that I'm his friend means so much, but it doesn't

mean that I shouldn't do anything about it."

"If he catches us talking like this, all alone, he will start thinking that something is happening between us, and you don't want to find out what would happen if he got suspicious."

"Let him get suspicious. It's not like I have friends of my own that wouldn't go up against him. If anything, he is the one that should be watching his back."

There was a moment of silence and I wondered what Barbara was thinking. She took another sip from her wine glass. She was still looking into my eyes, but every so often I could see her eyes turning up and down depending on which part of me she wanted to scrutinize more closely.

Barbara just couldn't hide how aroused she felt whenever she was with me, could she?

"I could be recording this and I could tell him about everything that you are saying. He would kill you in a heartbeat and the next time that I would see you would be in the cemetery."

I smiled. I knew that she could be so fiery when she wanted to, but I never thought that she would be saying those things right to my face. Even though the party was still going and the DJ had just turned up the music, my ears and my mind were ignoring everything that wasn't happening in this room.

"But that's the thing. I'm certain that you would never even think about doing something like that."

I couldn't stop thinking about how wrong this was, but it was for that reason that I felt my dick stirring in my pants. The only thing I wanted to do right now was to strip her naked, and it was such a pity that I couldn't. Barbara wouldn't let me – not yet, anyway.

"Don't test me like that. You could be surprised," she said, almost immediately turning and leaving, but I didn't let her. I grabbed her hand, which made her snap her head so that her eyes were looking into mine again.

I could almost read what she was thinking, and I pulled her closer to me, almost thinking that we were going to kiss. I could hear her breathing, I could hear everything that her body was doing, and I could even feel the warmth coming from it. It was intoxicating, and I was already addicted to it.

"What are you going to do now? Are you going to scream?" I asked, moving her a little bit closer to me. The more I did that, the more I tested her. I just wanted to find out if she was brave enough to destroy everything between me and my best friend.

The truth was that our friendship had been eroded a long time ago and now it was nothing more than a shell of its former self.

"I just might do something like that or I might kick you in the balls," she threatened, shaking her arm free.

I didn't like that she did that, but I wasn't going to be too forceful with her. And I was so content that she didn't move away from me right away. Barbara was actually doing the opposite. She stayed so close to me that I could still kiss her if I wanted to, but I wasn't certain if I should do that.

We had some chemistry together. Some good, intense chemistry and I knew that she was aware of that. In fact, it made me feel so certain about this, so certain that I wanted her no matter how much it would destroy everything that my life was about…

It was like time had frozen around us.

I put my hand on her waist this time. Like I said before, I wasn't going to be forceful any more than I already was. After all, I knew that Barbara wanted this to be happening.

It was for that reason that she wasn't moving away from me as quickly as she could.

In fact, it was for the same reason that she was even taking another step toward me. She could very well do what she said she was going to, which was to kick me in the balls, but I was certain she would never even try something like that.

Not to mention that I would see it coming and I would block her knee before it was too late. I just could never and would never see myself in such a shameful situation, where I would be hobbling in the main room where the party was taking place, my hands cupping my crotch.

Her lips were so close to me.

I could still hear her breathing.

Was she going to kiss me?

And just when I thought that she was going to, she turned around and left me after finishing her wine.

Fuck.

I knew that this was going to happen.

Every time that I thought we were going to kiss, she left me hanging.

I just couldn't wait any longer. I wanted to feel the sweetness of her lips kissing me, and she kept on teasing me.

What the hell was she thinking she was doing, always behaving so erratically with me?

I wasn't going to let things end this way. Not tonight and especially not when Pavel was getting piss drunk.

CHAPTER 3

Barbara

I knew that he was following me. When Igor had his mind set on something, he never stopped. That was why he was behind me and it was for the same reason he thought I was going to kiss him, even though I was certain I wasn't going to do that.

I checked the crowd at the party and I couldn't see my husband anymore. I wondered what he was doing.

Was it possible that he was kissing another woman? It was possible.

After all, when he was drunk, he wasn't his normal self. He was always so changed that I couldn't even recognize him and the more that happened, the more I realized I made a big mistake when I decided to marry him.

My father *had* told me that it was a mistake. He had warned me, but now it was pointless to be dwelling on what happened in the past.

What mattered was what was happening at this moment.

The house where the party was taking place wasn't big, and I was already feeling so stressed, thinking about my husband, his drinking, and his best friend hounding me.

I knew that he was staring at my ass. I was so certain about that that it was making me uncomfortable and a little turned on at the same time. Everything that happened before I married Pavel was happening again, wasn't it?

I had that man coming after me with all the power he had and it was turning me on. In fact, it was doing so much more than that, too. It hardened my nipples, something I thought would never happen because of him.

After all, he was supposed to be nothing more than a friend. But now I knew that he wanted so much more to happen between us.

I could just imagine him with his hands on my waist, turning me around in a heartbeat, and then cupping my cheeks before he kissed me.

What the hell was even going on in my mind? I thought, noticing that he was still coming after me even though I kept trying to lose him in the house.

I supposed I should be thankful that none of the guests were looking at us. They were all bikers. Some of them were women and some of them were men. They were all chatting loudly, laughing, joking, and the environment was so heavy that I just didn't want to be in here any longer than I had to be.

I wasn't born to be in a place like this.

The smoke in the air.

The smell of cheap marijuana.

Bikers sniffing lines of cocaine.

And pretty much everything else. It all made me think that I felt dirty just being here, even though I had decided to come here so that I didn't make my husband suspicious about what was going on.

I checked behind my shoulder one more time to make sure that Igor wasn't following me anymore, and I thought I had finally lost him, but then I realized that he was actually by my side.

He was by my side and with his arms crossed over his torso. I had no idea what he was thinking, but it felt… kind of good to have someone hounding me with so much vigor.

He was literally stalking me and I couldn't do anything about it – not without alerting everyone at the party to what was going on here.

I stopped where I was, saying under my breath, "What the hell do you think you're doing?"

"Don't think that it stopped just because you left. That look in your eyes… I could read everything you were thinking."

"If you could, then what the hell do you think you're doing? Nothing is going to happen between us. I don't like you that much, and now that you're doing this, I'm thinking that it was a mistake telling you so much about us."

"You might be right about that, but don't try fooling yourself. This isn't going to stop here. I just can't stand seeing Pavel getting piss drunk while you're all alone at the party."

And the more he said those things, the more I felt that he was in the right.

The only problem was that I just could never and would never let anything happen between us because I wasn't stupid.

Perhaps I was being too romantic about it and fantasizing about something that just wasn't true, but I didn't want to destroy my marriage so suddenly and after it started no more than a couple of months ago.

I wasn't lying about that. My marriage started about a couple months ago, and I still thought that it could be salvaged.

That was one of the reasons why I was so reluctant about what was going on between me and Igor, even though he was everything I wanted.

He made me feel safe when everything was going to shit between me and Pavel. He kept me protected and he always heard everything I had to say.

That was one of the reasons why I felt that my husband didn't value me as much as he should. He always treated me as his old lady, which I was, but I was also so much more than that.

I was more than his trophy for him to be showing around as though it was the most common thing to do and that it was okay to do that.

As if Igor could read what I was thinking, he opened the door that was by my side, and then we stepped out.

"I knew that you wanted to get out of the house and here I am facilitating that for you," he said with such a dirty smile on his face. It made me want to slap him on his face right now. I would even knock some teeth out of his mouth if I did that.

And yet, if I did something like that, it would be like ruining everything that I thought about Igor. I thought that he had a good heart even though he couldn't stop hitting on his best friend's wife.

Now that I was thinking about it, there really weren't friends in the biker 'universe,' was there? I always thought that they were like inseparable best buddies, but the longer this went on, the more I realized how stupid I had been.

Igor wanted me to be feeling conflicted about it.

He put his hand on the wall behind me and even though I could still escape him by running off the other way, I knew that I wouldn't.

I liked how controlling and obsessive he was.

He was doing this behind Pavel's back and couldn't at all feel conflicted about it.

All he knew was that it couldn't continue the way that it was. I couldn't keep thinking that everything would happen the way that my husband wanted it. He wanted me to have his baby, but I couldn't see myself letting that happen.

I thought that building a family was everything I wanted after turning 18, but it wasn't it.

I did kind of want it, but not in this way and not with someone that had said how much he hated my mom. She was in a coma, for fuck's sake! When I asked him to pay a part of the hospital bills, he said that he wanted to see her dead.

I guess that he said that because she'd bluntly told him that she didn't approve of the marriage. She thought that it wouldn't make me happy.

How right was she. Had I known that she was right about it I would have stopped my marriage before it was too late, but now it already was so.

I had this marriage ring on my finger and I couldn't do anything about it. I couldn't remove it.

In fact, if I did something like that, I would never forgive myself.

After all, my vows during the wedding were important to me. They were some of the most important things to me, and I didn't want to feel like I was betraying myself.

I put my hand on Igor's chest and I tried to move him away from me, but he didn't budge.

He actually stayed where he was and his eyes were examining mine. He was still trying to read what I was thinking and he knew everything, didn't he? He knew how much I wanted him to kiss me right now.

My broken marriage. My broken life. My mother in a coma, and pretty much every bad thing happening in my life – Igor could take care of everything.

He could cleanse my troubled life, and for that to happen, I only needed to let him kiss me.

And it just might happen now.

CHAPTER 4

Igor

Barbara was right in front of me and I had her cornered against the wall. I was doing this out of my own volition. Barbara was so stunning and her perfume was everything I wanted to be feeling right now.

Smelling.

Well, not just those things, but also everything about her.

It was as though time was moving in slow motion around us.

We knew where we were. We were just behind the house and Pavel could find us in the act. He could find us doing this and I was certain that the next thing he would do would be to pull out his gun and shoot me.

Even though he thought he was my friend, I knew that he would never let this slide.

He would kill me and he would feel extreme levels of remorse, but that would be about it.

"If my husband finds out about this, he will kill you," Barbara said and even though she was warning me, she knew that I already knew it. Her warning didn't mean anything to me.

Our lips were so close and I could finally do the thing that I had always wanted to do.

I had always wanted to kiss her and now was my opportunity.

"What does it matter if he tries to kill me? Even though he's the president of the club, nothing would matter anymore because he would find out that your heart isn't entirely his."

I was right about that. Pavel's heart would be shattered and there would be nothing he would be able to do about it. Was I being an asshole about this? I was, pretty much, but nothing could stop me right now.

I looked into her eyes, wondering what she was thinking. If Barbara wanted me to go on with this, then I was going to.

And the warmth of her body was so intoxicating I couldn't stop feeling it. I couldn't stop thinking about it, and I just wanted to be so close to her.

Our bodies were so close right now that our chests were almost touching. I noticed her breath hitching in her throat, and I knew that now was the opportunity that I was being so patient for.

I put my hand on her cheek and I lowered my head, connecting our lips. When they were touching, her body froze up.

Barbara couldn't help herself. She put her hand on my waist and brought me a little bit closer to her.

Now, our chests were finally touching and I could feel her breasts.

They were so incredibly warm.

I just wanted to have my hands all over them, and it was a pity that I couldn't make that happen right now.

After all, in case we noticed anyone coming this way, the next thing we would do would be to pretend that we were only talking.

Her lips were so sweet. They were tender, wet, and so hungry for more of me. Our kiss was passionate and she was showing me how much she had been wanting for this to happen since we first met.

Of course, I couldn't know that last part for sure, but something about it still showed me that it was the truth.

And as time went on, I also found out that I couldn't control my feelings for her.

This whole time, I thought that I would finally find someone different, someone that wasn't forbidden, but that was the thing, wasn't it? What was forbidden turned me on.

And that was why I was doing this.

I didn't know it was love, but I was obsessed. I just couldn't stop thinking about Barbara.

I put my hand on her shirt, lifting it up. I could feel her belly and how soft and smooth her skin was.

It was everything I wanted to be feeling right now.

I moved my hand further up and I thought that she was going to let me feel her breasts, but then she moved away from me in a heartbeat. I didn't even have time to react and grab her hand.

One moment she was kissing me and the next she was scurrying away from me as quickly as she could.

I was disappointed, but I couldn't say that I didn't see it coming.

I lifted my hand, trying to take her to me again, but I knew that it wouldn't be so easy.

After all, Barbara was with her back turned to me, and I knew that what just happened affected her deeply.

"Barbara, I don't know exactly what you're thinking right now, but I do know that there's no point in lying to yourself."

I approached her, putting myself right behind her. I had my hands on her shoulders and I thought that she was going to whirl around and slap me, but she didn't.

She did turn around slowly and I saw the tears coming out of her eyes. She was crying and I didn't know what to do.

I had always thought that she was so incredibly strong, but now she was showing me a side of her that I didn't think she had.

After all, even when she vented to me about what was going on in her life and how Pavel wasn't treating her fairly, she was always so strong. She always talked about it as though it wasn't affecting her much.

But now she was crying and I knew that she had so much to tell me.

"I want to be somewhere that isn't here," she said and I nodded. There was no point in delaying what was inevitable. She wanted to go somewhere with me, and that was fine.

I didn't have a house like Pavel had, but I had a small

apartment on the outskirts of the city. The place was small but homey. She would feel right at home there, especially because it wouldn't be the first time that she was there with me.

This should be something that should be making me think a lot about what was going on.

After all, even if we managed to be together after dealing with Pavel, then what? What would happen then? Could I trust Barbara that she wouldn't do the same she was doing to her husband but with someone else?

I didn't know, but right now there was no time to be thinking about those things.

My motorcycle was behind the house as well and I was thankful for that. It wasn't that I had planned on leaving the party with her on my motorcycle, but I was thankful that I had the opportunity to do that without anyone finding out who my partner was.

She was going to put on a helmet and they would never know that it was her. After all, it was dark and most of the people at the party were piss drunk. They were most likely going to think that she was just another guest that had cozied up to me and that now I was going to take her home.

She climbed on the motorcycle behind me and put her arms around my torso. Even though we weren't lovers – at least, that wasn't what I was thinking – it felt so right to have her arms around me and feel her big breasts pressed against my back.

This moment was so good that I didn't want it to end, even though I was aware that it had to. *All good things come to an end, don't they?*

It was difficult to be thinking clearly right now, and my cock was just so hard in my pants. It was going to be difficult to be riding with such a boner showing, but there was nothing that I could do about it.

Barbara wanted to go with me and she was going to. I was going to take her to a place where she was going to feel more comfortable.

In the meantime, I was promising myself that this wasn't

going to take long. I had just looked at the side and found her husband spread out in the front yard, so drunk that he'd already passed out, a broken beer bottle by his side.

What a loser, I thought. I couldn't help but wonder why all the other members of the biker club thought that he was fit to be our leader. I sure as hell thought that he wasn't.

I turned on the engine of the motorcycle and it roared to life. I felt Barbara tightening her arms around me as though she wanted to be feeling even safer than she was.

And after looking over my shoulder one more time to make sure that nobody was looking, we took off. I couldn't wait until I was with her in my apartment.

I was going to be the husband tonight that her true husband couldn't be.

CHAPTER 5

Barbara

I didn't know what I was doing in his apartment. It was small, but there was something about it that was exactly like Igor. A little rough-looking, dirty, smelly, but still remarkably homey. Maybe it was the blandness and how functional it was. It had nothing more than what he needed, and he wasn't the kind of guy to stay inside it for long.

I just felt right at home being here, and I was certain that was exactly one of the reasons why he took me here.

I told him that I needed to go to a place different from that house where the party was taking place, and it was indeed so much better to be here.

Much more silent, too, even though the upstairs neighbor was blasting music as he sang alongside it. I didn't know why he thought he was doing something that other people were appreciating, and his voice was like nails scratching a blackboard.

Just listening to it was enough to make me feel like puking.

Igor was sitting in front of me and across the other side of the coffee table, which was a surprise.

I was surprised that he had a coffee table in his living room. Was it right to even call it a living room, though? I didn't know, but it was so small that it was connected to the kitchen, which was also nothing more than a small hallway.

Still, for someone like Igor, it was more than good enough.

He was looking at me with questioning eyes. I knew what he was thinking. After sitting down and him giving me a glass with whiskey in it, he was wondering if I was finally going to say something.

I bit my lower lip.

How was I even going to approach the avalanche of problems that I had? There were so many of them that I felt overwhelmed, and there was nothing I could do about it.

Nothing more than confiding in him some of it. Even though I trusted Igor a lot, this was still so difficult.

I took a deep breath and he put down the beer can that he was drinking from. Even though we were both still drinking, we weren't drunk – at least, not yet.

I always knew when I was drunk and now it was no different.

"It's just my mother. The more I think about her, the more I begin to realize that there's nothing I can do about her. I just don't have the money to pay for the treatment she really needs, and I know that I can work as hard as possible and it would never be enough."

He took a deep breath, entwining his fingers on his lap. He was hunched over, his arms on his legs.

The way he was looking at me, he really showed me that he cared about what was going on here.

"It's okay to be worried about your mother, and I know how shitty it has been for you. I know that Pavel should be doing more."

He really should be. And for starters, he should have never said what he said about it. He should never have said that he wanted to see my mom dead. That was just unforgivable, and it made me want to hate him even more than I already did, something I didn't think possible.

I bit my bottom lip harder. Should I really tell Igor about that as well?

I decided that I should. After all, he was being so much more than my friend right now. Much more than my best friend, even. He was the only person that I felt I could tell everything about.

"And he also said that he wanted to see my mother dead. Every time that I think about it, that I remember his words, I think about how much I hate him, and I don't think it's something I could ever change."

He widened his eyes the moment that I said that. And everything was so quiet around us that I could almost hear his breathing. I noticed him balling his right hand. What I just said really made him furious and if my husband was right here with us, nothing good would happen.

I was so certain about it that my heart was tight just thinking about it.

"He really said that?" He asked, standing up. "It's unforgivable and you know it."

He walked around the coffee table, sitting on the couch where I was sitting. He was a bit closer to me now and I could feel his leg touching mine, which sent goosebumps through my body. I vowed to myself not to tell him anything about that.

Even though we had just kissed, I didn't want it to be anything more than that. I didn't want him to think that I really was thinking about cheating on my husband, even though… that kind of already happened.

He grabbed my hand and I replied, "He did that and a lot worse. I thought that he was going to hit me. I thought that he really loved me, but then he was behaving like he was going to hurt me. I never thought that asking him for help with the hospital bills was going to make him so angry."

"It's just like you said to me once. He doesn't like your mother because she said she didn't want you to marry him, and now I can see how right she was."

"You're right about that, but I still want to think that there's something I can do to salvage the marriage. Do you think I'm right about that?" I asked, feeling his finger moving over the back of my hand. Now that he was doing that, he was making me realize that even though he was a biker, he could be caring when he wanted to.

He shook his head, put his hand on my cheek, and made me kiss him once again.

This time, I didn't do anything to try and stop him. I knew that it would be pointless. I actually wanted him to kiss me, and he was giving me that and a lot more.

I had been thinking about this for such a long time and I felt that I was finally ready for the 'next stage,' so to speak.

I kissed him again and then I said, "Please take away all the bad things going on in my life right now. Please make me forget about them, even if only for a short while."

He looked into my eyes, brushing his finger on my cheek.

"I'm going to do that and a lot more," Igor promised me, pushing me so that I was lying on the couch and he was on top of me.

He blocked some of the lamp light coming from the ceiling, and I was really feeling so much better that I could feel all the bad thoughts plaguing my mind going away.

And then, his lips came crashing down on me, kissing me. They were as sweet as I remembered, and also just as hot. They took away all the breath in my lungs, and suddenly breathing got a lot harder.

Igor was so much more passionate this time as well.

So much hotter.

So much more virile.

Igor held nothing back, his hands moving under my shirt and lifting it. I couldn't do anything about it until it was too late. Until my shirt was over my head and he was finally looking at my exposed breasts.

Even though I still had my bra on, I felt like they were exposed.

He was just looking at them.

Examining them.

Stretching this moment for a lot longer than it should be.

And it was then that I decided to make the best decision of my life.

I was going to make this moment about me and not us.

I could already feel his hand moving over my belly, examining it. And of course, for someone like Igor, just doing that wasn't enough.

He needed more.

Oh, so much more.

No wonder he reached up and then around me, lifting me ever so slightly. He pulled the hook and my breasts were free. And then, so slowly, he peeled it off.

Like it wasn't even there.

My bosoms were utterly exposed now and he could see everything. Igor was enjoying what he was seeing, and I could tell that by the way that he was looking at me.

His eyes were full of lust for me.

And perhaps even something much more than that. Perhaps he was even feeling love for me, but I didn't think that was the case.

I'd better not think that it was. After all, I just didn't want to make the same mistake as before.

I didn't want to fall in love with another biker. I knew how much that would hurt me.

CHAPTER 6

Barbara

And yet, it was still happening, wasn't it? His hands were all over me. He was exploring every part of me, and there was nothing I could do about it.

I mean, there was something I could do, but I wasn't going to.

I just loved this moment and how it was happening.

Now that my breasts were fully exposed, Igor could do anything he wanted to them.

Thus, it wasn't surprising when he started to pinch and squeeze them with his fingers, making me arch my back. His fingers grazing on my nipples was everything I thought it was going to be.

I couldn't help but wonder when it was the last time that I felt so happy. It was probably when I thought I still was going to have a good life with my husband.

Igor was showing me how much I was missing this whole time.

His hands massaged my boobs.

He fumbled with them.

I felt his fingers applying pressure in all the right spots. He knew what he was doing, and the lust in his eyes was something I would never forget.

It was like everything had slowed down around me, around us, and I just couldn't see myself doing anything different. It was for that reason that I just had to wrap my legs around him, and then I pulled him down so that I could feel his boner pressing against my pussy.

Like hell that I was going to let him have me naked without him doing the same for me. Igor studied my eyes and he knew that I wanted him to do the same for me. I wanted him to strip naked for me, and I knew that he was going to grant my wish.

He stopped kissing me for a brief moment and then he put his fingers under his shirt, lifting it. It was the first time that I was seeing his chest without his shirt, and it sent shivers down my spine.

I knew he was perfect, but I didn't think it was going to make my jaw drop.

Rippling muscles.

Bulging biceps.

Scary tattoos.

Was there anything about Igor that didn't show me how much I had always wanted to make this moment happen?

I didn't think so.

He smiled without showing his teeth, showing me how devilish his smile was.

"Like what you're seeing, Barbara?" He asked and I could almost slap his face again. It wasn't like his question was a true question. It was more of a rhetorical one, and I was certain that he was aware of that.

After all, it was for that reason that he wasn't smiling right now.

In the meantime, I just couldn't help myself. I shoved my fingers under his waistband and pulled down his pants, and then he wriggled himself out of them. He was quite clumsy doing that, and I didn't expect any differently.

But when Igor was out of his pants, I felt like I was in heaven.

He was only with his boxer briefs on, and it was a black pair. His bulge was nothing short of huge, and it made me want to touch it. He already had quite the boner, and if we were going until the end with this, I now couldn't help but wonder if he would be able to fit it inside of me.

Would he?

I didn't know, but the question hung in the air and I just couldn't do anything about it.

I mean, I could do something about it, but I didn't know if I wanted to.

I started to massage his legs. His torso. His pecs. His biceps, and pretty much every part of his body. There was just something about it that turned me on so much, and I knew exactly what that was.

Enough with all the teasing, I thought, finally putting my fingers under his pair of boxer briefs and then lowering it.

Now, I could finally see his prick.

It looked quite mean and it was pointing at me. My finger brushed over the tip, and I felt his body shuddering. He was doing everything not to come right now, wasn't he? I asked myself, but it was pointless to even try to answer it.

The answer was more than obvious. Igor was indeed doing that, and it made me feel flattered. I just never thought that I would see another man so turned on for me.

He lowered his head one more time, kissing me.

His lips lingered on mine for what felt like an eternity. He wasn't moving away.

I felt his tongue going between my lips, and I just couldn't fight against it. I felt it breaching inside, fighting against my tongue, and then he had full control over the kiss. Igor could do anything he wanted to me right now and I just would never be able to do anything about it.

It was like the kiss was going to last forever. Breathing was even more difficult than before, and I felt how sweaty my body was. It was covered by a layer of sweat. I was going to need a quick, cold shower after we were done.

His fingers played with my boobs again, grazing over my nipples.

Igor didn't hold anything back, wrapping his lips around my nipples.

He sucked on them for what felt like an eternity.

Igor then turned me around slowly when he felt he had me exactly the way he wanted me. I lifted my butt so that it was pointing to his cock, and I could feel how much he wanted to penetrate me right now.

He pulled his body slightly closer so that I could feel his cock nudging my orifice. Was he really going to penetrate me without a condom? I asked myself, and it was like he'd just read my mind.

As soon as I finished thinking that, I heard him picking up his pair of pants. It was lying on the floor and he didn't need to stretch his arm much to pick it up.

With it in his hands, he fished out of the right pocket a condom. He ripped it out of the package, put it on his prick, and then took his time, finally penetrating me.

Was he planning on fucking tonight or did he always go around prepared for sex? I didn't know, but either option added to his sexiness.

As he did that, he held me by grabbing my hair.

I couldn't do anything about it. I didn't want to be a bother to the neighbors, so I didn't scream much. Igor was stretching me so much, and it was as painful as I'd thought.

He was so much bigger.

And then he leaned down, his lips close to my ears. For a moment, I thought that he was going to slip his tongue inside my ear canal – something I was certain didn't even make any sense - but which still crossed my mind.

"You're never going to forget tonight, Barbara," he promised me and I felt shivers running down my spine. I knew he was going to say that and it still affected me that much.

Then, without giving me a warning, he started to pound in and out of me, doing exactly what he had just promised me. I would never forget tonight.

My body started to match his thrust for thrust, and I loved the pace that he was employing. It wasn't too fast or slow. It was just the right speed.

When it wasn't as painful as before and I was better used to his size, he increased his pace and it was so much better. I could finally let go of everything bad going on in my life.

Didn't have to think about those things anymore.

Igor leaned down so that his lips were close to my right ear again. He was going to ask me a question and I didn't know if I was going to like it. It just might shatter everything happening now.

"Wanna run away with me tonight? I promise you that Pavel wouldn't be able to find us. I could find a way to pay for all the hospital bills your mom needs, and then I would find a way to deal with your husband. I'm not saying that I would kill him, but I know that I would do something about it." He took a deep breath, his body still pounding against me. I hadn't come yet, waiting until he did so that we came at the same time. "Plus, I'm kind of tired of the Punishers. I think I want something different for my life."

And now the problem was that I had no idea if I should even answer that question.

After all, what was he thinking I was going to say about it? That I was going to run away with him and abandon my husband?

It was tempting, but there wasn't much time to be thinking about it right now.

My body started to convulse and I could feel his prick throbbing inside of me. Igor was coming and so was I. Nothing better than this.

We were coming at the same time and even though I knew it would never happen, I wanted his baby. I never gave Pavel one, but I still wanted Igor's baby.

Building a family with him.

That would be nice.

CHAPTER 7

Igor

The next morning, I wasn't surprised when I woke up and I looked at what was around me, not finding my muse. I thought that I was going to find her lying on my bed by my side, but she was nowhere to be seen, and it was to be expected.

At least I could still smell her perfume in the bedroom.

It was good. It filled my lungs, making me want more of her, and it was such a pity that it would never happen.

I thought that I was finally going to do it. I thought that I was finally going to leave the Punishers, but it didn't happen. I just didn't want to be anywhere far from Barbara, and could anyone ever fault me for thinking that way about it?

Obviously not.

Something interesting began to happen after that night with her. Barbara started to avoid me more and more, even during the parties that the Punishers threw. I had thought that they meant we would have more opportunities to fuck, but she always avoided me so much that I just gave up on that.

Could anyone ever fault me for doing that, too? For thinking that way about it?

Obviously not, but it still didn't help with the way I started to feel about everything going on in my life.

I really thought that I would never fall in love with anyone, but after spending so much time with Barbara, getting to know her, understanding her problems, hearing her talking about them, and pretty much everything else, I just wanted to be with her.

I had even woken up one morning wondering what it would be like to have a family with her, something that had never crossed my mind until then.

Shit. What the hell was even going on in my mind? I didn't know, but I just wanted it to go away. I couldn't even function properly. Couldn't be the biker that I was. Couldn't ride in the city without thinking about Barbara all the time, and that was just not good.

I shook my head, riding down the road on my motorcycle. I wasn't thinking about Barbara right now, but the moment that my eyes found her on the sidewalk, I knew that it was her.

It had been so long since the last time we had seen each other.

I didn't know that she had changed so much.

She was walking out of a store with a couple of bags. When her eyes found me, they went wide. The last person she thought she was going to stumble on here was me, and that was obvious.

Barbara looked so flustered she didn't even know what she was doing.

She was just there, frozen on the spot.

I stopped my motorcycle by her side. It was a calm, sunny day. Not much happening. Some people were in the streets, crossing the sidewalks, but other than that, we were pretty much alone.

I could even feel and hear the wind swirling around us.

I never thought that Barbara had changed so much to the point that she now had a huge belly. Her body was still about the same, but her belly was much bigger.

What happened after that night? I wanted to ask her that question. I wanted to know what was going on in her mind, but I didn't even know if that was even the right thing to do right now.

I was confused, and yet I wasn't going to let this continue its course. I couldn't.

I stopped my motorcycle. I put my foot on the ground and took off my helmet. I made her look in my eyes and she was. She was frozen where she was, but she was telling me so much about her reaction, about how she was feeling about this.

"Long time no see," I said and I thought she was going to say something, but for the next few seconds, she just remained dead silent. So silent she was like a ghost.

When I realized that she really wasn't going to say anything, I decided to say, "Looks like you are pregnant now. *Congratulations.* I think you deserve some happiness, especially considering everything you're going through."

And after hearing that, it was no surprise that she was going to be acting like she didn't know what I was even talking about.

I couldn't help but check her bags again. Just a glance. They were heavy and looked full. She bought all of that just for the baby? I asked myself, feeling like not externalizing it. I didn't think that there was a point.

After all, if she was pregnant with Pavel's baby, then I had nothing to do with it.

I was going to be happy for her… Right?

I shook my head, looking to the other side, the road in front of me. There was no point in going on with this. Why was I even still thinking about Barbara when she made everything so clear? She didn't want to see me and she thought that what we had that night was a mistake.

She took some steps toward me. I looked at her again and I could feel her pain. It was in her eyes, and yet after doing that she just left me and kept on avoiding me this whole time, I just couldn't say anything about it. I couldn't do anything about it so that she felt better.

"It's not his baby," she said and my eyes went wide in a moment.

I figured that there was something odd about her pregnancy, but I never thought that she was just going to outright say that the baby wasn't Pavel's. What the hell? What the hell was going on here?

I didn't know, but what she just said shook me to the core.

I got off my motorcycle right away. I put my hand on her shoulder and led her to the alleyway behind her. She came with me without protesting about it, and I was happy about that.

I thought that she was going to refuse to be alone with me. I thought that she was going to start to scream and screech, but she didn't.

When we were alone, I finally felt like I could ask her about everything that happened.

"What did you just say?" I asked, trying to keep my voice tone as low as possible so that the passerby didn't get suspicious. Some people walked behind the entrance of the alleyway and never looked where we were, something that relieved me.

"I said the baby isn't his," she affirmed as she continued to stare at me. I could feel her determination, but I could also feel that she was feeling something else.

Something that she was holding back, and I had no idea for how much longer she could keep that up.

"Barbara, what's going on?" I growled, cornering her against the wall.

Then, I noticed the tears coming out and I couldn't do anything about it. They just started coming out, she was crying and sobbing, and the only thing I could do at the moment was to put my arms around her, which I did.

I was hugging her where everybody could see us, and I didn't care.

If Pavel ever found out about this, it wouldn't matter. Nothing would matter because I was beginning to understand what was going on here.

I didn't think that she had had an affair with anyone else, which meant that the baby could only be mine.

And that thought froze me.

Was I really going to become a father? If I was going to, it changed everything. I wouldn't know what to do, or perhaps I was mistaken and I already knew what to do.

That crazy proposal that I had made the last time we were together before now...

Running away with her somewhere else. Somewhere that wasn't Las Vegas. Maybe even to the other side of the country, where we could have a good life together and wouldn't have to worry about the Punishers.

Still, I couldn't help but wonder if she would always be paranoid that Pavel was going to come after us.

I could kill him, but that would only bring more complications.

Gleb had never been the leader they wanted, but Pavel was different. They all thought that he was going to turn everything around for us, make everything better and that the Punishers were finally going to return to their days of glory.

They were so blind to what was going on but knowing that didn't change anything.

Barbara looked up, finding my eyes.

"We are leaving and going to New York City. I know it's a long trip, but it's what we need. I know that the baby is mine and, over there, we can finally start doing that thing I had proposed when we were together in my apartment."

And I thought that Barbara was going to protest, but the way she was looking into my eyes told me it was what she wanted as well.

She wanted me as part of her family, too.

CHAPTER 8

Barbara

It had been a long trip. I wasn't going to deny it. It was such a long trip I thought we would never make it. But we were now in New York City, and it was a city so much bigger than I thought it actually was.

In here, we had a life so much better than what we had in Las Vegas. Igor started to work as a security guard, and he made enough money to keep us afloat.

And also enough to pay for my mom's hospital bills. We weren't having a life of luxury, but it was so much better than what I had with Pavel, who didn't even want to pay for my mom's hospital bills when I was still with him.

Just thinking about that, I couldn't help but feel my blood boiling. He was – had been, I corrected myself – my husband and couldn't even do the one thing that I needed from him.

But there was no point in remembering what happened. *What had happened.* It was now all in the past and I could look ahead at the life I had here.

Igor and I lived in an apartment building as well. Nothing special about it. The kind of place where we could have a good life without being bothered by other people.

Some of the neighbors were noisy and I wasn't going to deny that, but I could tolerate them. No place would ever be perfect.

And one of the good things about this moment in my life was

that I finally had my baby. I was holding her in my arms. My baby girl. I couldn't imagine my life without her.

I had thought that having a baby would destroy my life.

How wrong I had been about that.

She was so cute.

I was holding her in my arms and walking on the sidewalk. I had thought that taking a walk with her was going to be good for her, and it was working.

Ann couldn't stop looking around, checking all the buildings with her curious eyes.

She mumbled something, but couldn't pronounce the word. Was she going to say that the buildings were beautiful? I didn't know, but I knew that it was something along those lines.

She moved her arms around as though she wanted to touch the buildings, but I knew it was silly to think about it that way.

I looked in the distance and I noticed the stormy clouds coming this way. Even though I knew I didn't have any control over it, I just wanted tonight to be a clear one.

So, no rain. No nothing. Just a calm, solitary night where I could lie down in my bed and fall asleep.

Ann could make me so busy some nights. I knew that she didn't do it on purpose, but there were so many nights when she cried and we couldn't do much other than get up, put her in our arms, and rock her, hoping that it was going to calm her mind.

But right now, she looked so charming, mumbling, clenching her hands, looking at me and then at the buildings, making me wonder what she was thinking at the moment.

And I also couldn't help but feel a shiver of paranoia in me. I couldn't do anything about it.

Ever since leaving Pavel, I knew that he was still thinking about me.

But the thing was that we fled all the way over to the other side of the country, where we were certain he would never find us.

Plus, New York City was much different from Las Vegas. In here, the police were a constant, present force. If the Punishers showed up here, we were certain that they would be caught.

Not to mention that it would mean it would be the end of the club itself, something I was certain not even someone like Pavel wanted.

If there was something more important to him than me, it was the success of his motorcycle club.

That was why I was certain he would never show up.

Still, I couldn't help but stop and look over my shoulder when I thought I had heard the sound of his motorcycle in the distance. I really was getting so paranoid about my life here, wasn't I? I asked myself, looking at my baby again.

Would it ever change? I didn't know, but I supposed that it didn't matter.

I knew that Igor was at the nightclub where he was working. He had just gone there. Most nights I was alone, but during the daytime, he was always around. Still, he looked for more work.

He said it was difficult, but that he was looking for a second job so that he could continue to support my mom better.

One other thing I was still paranoid about was Pavel going after my family, but so far, he hadn't even attempted to do anything about them. I knew that he still wanted to find me, though.

After all, the first few days after we crossed the border out of Nevada state, he called me so many times that I ended up having to replace my phone chip.

Thankfully, he didn't know my new number.

I took a deep breath in, finally reaching my apartment. I had just finished my walk outside with Ann and the only thing I wanted to do right now was to put her to sleep after giving her something to eat. And I had just the thing in mind. Tonight, I was going to make her favorite dinner.

And I knew she was excited about it. It was like she could read my mind.

"Tonight, I'm going to make you your favorite," I said, pinching her right cheek slightly.

She started to giggle and shake her arms gently. I entered my apartment building, took the elevator to the fifth floor, and then entered my apartment itself.

When I closed the door after turning around, I noticed that I wasn't alone.

I froze up on the spot, not knowing what to do. I was seeing the shadow of a person joining with mine. The light coming from the window was behind him.

It was just one person. Just one man, and if he was a low-level criminal that had come here to rob me, then I could fight against him. I wasn't saying that it would be easy, but I still could.

I turned around slowly, finding him.

When my eyes processed who he was, I froze up again.

I never thought that he would come, much less that he would find where I lived. He was, of course, none other than Pavel, and he had his arms crossed over his chest, looking changed. I didn't know what had happened to him since I fled from the Punishers, but it was more obvious that he was suffering this whole time because of that.

He also knew that the baby was his, so maybe it had something to do with that, too.

His eyes were bloodshot. He was looking at me as though he was thinking about killing me, but I would never let something like that happen. I knew that my baby couldn't live without me, and nothing and no one would ever change that.

He stepped toward me, and I recoiled.

"Pavel? What do you think you're doing? I thought I made it clear when I fled from the Punishers. I don't want to be with you anymore. You said you hated my mother and that you weren't going to help pay her hospital bills, and I can never forgive you for that. It's only thanks to Igor that she's still alive and that there's still a chance that she's going to wake up from her coma."

"I don't really care about that, bitch. I came here for my baby, and you are going to give her to me. She's important to me. She's much more to me than you will ever be, and as for your mother... I stand by what I said. I want to see her dead."

And then, I screamed. It was the only thing I could do. He was much bigger than me and he could beat me to a pulp and I wouldn't be able to do anything about it.

The only thing I could hope for right now was either one of the neighbors helping me or Igor showing up all of a sudden.

And I needed to keep Ann far from him no matter what.

CHAPTER 9

Igor

I was getting off my motorcycle, thinking about two people only. My wife, Barbara, and my baby, Ann. They were both special to me. I had once thought that I would never build a family with anyone, but now I could see how wrong I had been about that.

Having a family was everything I wanted.

It was raining outside, but the rain wasn't heavy. It wetted my clothes, but I was already getting off my motorcycle anyway and I was going to enter the apartment building where we lived. There was nothing special about it. It wasn't run down or anything of the sort, and it actually looked clean most of the time.

Anyway, those things didn't matter right now.

There was something that I was concerned about. I had thought that Barbara was going to text me to say that everything was okay here. She always did to make sure that I didn't get worried, but throughout the night this time, she didn't. We couldn't and we would never take our safety here lightly.

I wish I could tell the police that there was a biker club trying to hurt us, but I couldn't. I could never involve the police in what was happening here. Just didn't trust them – at all.

I took a deep breath in, taking the elevator to the fifth floor. I opened the door and the first thing I noticed was that Barbara was on the other side of the living room, her back against the wall, and sitting on the floor.

She was crying.

She had her arms around her legs, pushing them against her.

Seeing that, I had to run up to her right away. I put my hand on her knee and shook it slightly. "Barbara, what happened here?" I asked, looking around me and noticing that the living room looked like a mess.

It looked as though there had been a fight. If so, who had she fought against? And who had dared to hurt her? There was only one person that I was suspicious about. One person crazy enough to do something like that.

This was New York City and this neighborhood was supposed to be safe, but we were still new here. We hadn't antagonized anyone and we never would. Whoever had trashed the place and hurt my wife was someone that knew us, and they knew us well.

She finally looked up, finding my eyes. I looked as worried as she did, and my blood boiled, seeing this. The only thing I wanted to do right now was to punch to a pulp whoever had done this.

They weren't going to get away with it.

"It's Pavel," she answered, breaking down again. As soon as her first sob came out, I put my arms around her, pushing her against my body so that she felt safe and comfortable.

And yet, it wasn't enough.

The next thought that crossed my mind was where my baby was. If Pavel was the one behind this, then he had to have come for Ann, and if he had stolen her from us, I would never forgive him.

He would pay for what he did with his life.

Barbara looked up, finding my eyes. They were bloodshot. I brushed her forehead with my hand, making sure that I was doing everything so that she felt better.

Still, it wasn't working.

It was never going to be enough because she needed Ann right now and I knew it meant that asshole had taken her from us. Just thinking about that, I felt my blood boiling even hotter than before so much I thought I was going to start a killing spree.

I could kill everyone in the city right now.

"And Ann… He took her as well," she said, but right now she didn't need to say that. I could already retrace everything that happened here.

Barbara had her arms wrapped around herself, and her overwhelming sadness and distress were the only reasons why I hadn't run out of the apartment yet, looking for Pavel wherever he was. I had no idea where he was, but if he was here in New York City, despite how vast it was, I was certain I could sniff him out.

"I know and I'm going to find him no matter what. I'm going to kill him and I'm going to save our baby. Nothing can never and will never change that."

She was with her hands clasped in front of her as though she was praying. It was the first time I was seeing her doing that. Barbara was a strong woman, and it just wasn't like her to show weakness.

I turned around slowly, checking my gun on my waist. It was there, and I knew I was going to need it. One of the good things about living here in New York City was that I made new friends.

I knew they were going to help me.

They knew about some of my story, some of my past, and they were going to be with me, and they were also going to help me.

My hand was shaking, but it was okay.

It wasn't the first time that I was feeling so nervous.

I had to smoke now. I had to do something that made me feel calmer, even if only a little.

Right now, I needed something to help me with this.

Thus, after making the call to my friends and telling them that I was going to need their help, the next thing I did was take a cigarette out of the pack I was holding in my hands.

I lit it up with a lighter, put it back in the pocket of my pants, and then hopped onto my motorcycle. I turned on the engine and I was going to ride off when I felt something grabbing my hand.

Or rather, it was someone.

Barbara.

We hadn't felt so connected as we were now. She was telling me so much with her eyes. The tears on her cheeks, her shaky hands, her bloodshot eyes.

Everything about her was telling me how much she needed my help right now, and it was exactly for that reason I was here.

I put my hand on her cheek, saying, "It doesn't matter what happens, I'm going to come back with Ann in my arms. Nobody can ever hurt us like this without suffering the consequences."

And then, I kissed her.

Barbara kissed me back, still holding my hand. I knew why she was doing that. She was worried about me, wasn't she? She was thinking that something terrible was going to happen to me.

While she could be worried, she didn't need to be.

It wasn't like I hadn't been in a similar situation before. That was part of the life of a biker. Her lips were incredibly sweet, and I knew I was going to miss them, even though I wasn't going to be away for long.

I had no idea where Pavel was, but I was going to find him. He could actually be fleeing back to Las Vegas at this moment, but even if that were the case, it wouldn't be enough to stop me. If I had to ride all the way over there on my motorcycle, then I was going to.

She was looking into my eyes as she said, "Just make sure that you come back safe and with Ann with you. I don't want to lose you. I don't want to lose either of you, and I feel like I would die without you."

I kissed her one more time. This might as well be the last time we were seeing each other together, but of course that wasn't what I was thinking about right now.

The only thing I was thinking about was when I would actually come back here so that I could spend more time with her.

And it wasn't like I had my fill of kissing her. I needed more, of course.

So much more.

And yet, I still had a mission to finish right now. Thus, it was with that thought in mind that I took off, thinking about just one thing – getting rid of Pavel no matter what.

No matter what he was thinking he was doing, he wasn't going to get away with it.

CHAPTER 10

Igor

I was outside and with my men. They were behind me on their motorcycles. Someone looking at us from afar would think that we were a motorcycle club, but that wasn't the case. The thought had crossed my mind before, though. I had thought about building another motorcycle club, but I just didn't have time for that sort of thing and I wasn't certain that I would ever want to do something like that.

After all, building another motorcycle club from scratch was difficult.

Not to mention that, at the moment, I had my job as a security guard and it was good enough.

It was dark and the moon was high in the sky, rising over the buildings. It was raining as well. The stormy clouds in the distance that I had seen before had told me that it was going to be raining, and the rain was now battering the city. It was nothing more than a drizzle until not too long ago.

I took a deep breath in.

I knew that Pavel and the rest of the Punishers were waiting for me. They were waiting for me because they knew I was going to come. They even knew I had already come here.

We were just outside of a large, residential, and abandoned apartment building. Even though all the lights were turned off, I could see some shadows moving in the rooms.

When we got inside, I didn't know if I would be able to come back to life.

This could very well be the last time that I was seeing the moonlight. Everyone was tense, of course. I should be getting out of the rain as soon as possible, but it was far from one of my most immediate concerns right now. The only thing I wanted to do was to actually storm into the building, start to kill everyone, and then save my daughter.

She was the most important thing to me right now, other than going back to my wife.

And here I had thought that the drunk clients in the nightclub were the worst thing that involved my life here.

How little I knew.

I took a deep breath in and I got off my motorcycle. They weren't shooting at me yet because they wanted me inside the trap that they had set up for me. It was going to be bloody, wasn't it? I could feel the tension in the air.

I headed inside with my men and then I knocked the door down. As soon as I was inside, the shootout started, and I killed my first man since leaving the Punishers.

Another shot.

And then another.

I was hiding behind a wall, but even then, I felt it wasn't enough.

I felt that when I got unlucky, one of those bullets would hit me and I would die.

A bullet just whizzed past my ear. Jesus. I thought I was going to die. In other circumstances, I would've thought that I would be dealing with this kind of situation much better than I was at the moment, but that wasn't what was happening.

I was actually tenser than I'd ever been. I was so anxious that I thought that I was going to have a heart attack. But perhaps that was what was making the difference at the moment for me.

Being so anxious was helping with my attention, and I was so focused I couldn't think about anything else. It was like a shot of adrenaline that never worn off, and I was pumped, seeing one guy falling after the other.

Was I really destroying the entire MC? All of the Punishers?

I didn't know, but I wasn't worried about it right now.

I had just made my way further inside the building and I reached the basement.

A stray thought that just crossed my mind. What if I had already killed Pavel and didn't notice it? It was possible, but I didn't want to think about that.

I reached another room in the basement and in this one I could see the two people I had come here for.

Pavel and my baby. She was in a stroller that he had brought for her. I knew that he thought it was his baby, and I was beginning to think I could finally understand the true weight of this situation.

My men were with me. They were behind me. Some of them were, at least. I knew that I was going to lose some soldiers in the shootout, but they all knew what could happen here when they came here with me.

They all understood the consequences.

I thought that I was going to find Pavel pointing his gun at my daughter's head, but that wasn't what he was doing. He was behind the crib, but he was actually pointing his gun at his head instead.

Was he really going to shoot himself? I didn't know, but seeing his face, the bloodshot eyes, the scars, and the lines of dried tears on his cheeks... I could tell that he was going through a lot.

I knew that his wife leaving him with me would hit him hard, but I thought he was stronger than this.

I thought that he was a better man.

"She's my wife and she left with you. I don't know what happened. You always said that I'm your best friend, and you did this to me. You killed the Punishers, and I'm the last one still alive."

I thought I was going to come down here and fight him. I thought that I was going to beat him to a pulp, but now I could see that there was no point in doing any of that anymore.

No point in kicking a dead dog.

"Lower your gun and get out of here before I change my mind. I don't want to think that I'm making a mistake, but there's no point in killing you. I can see that the worst punishment you can receive is actually living and knowing that your *ex-wife* doesn't really like you anymore. She told me about everything you were doing, how much you hated her mother, and that you didn't want to pay her hospital bills. Even though I don't have much money, I'm helping her however I can, and so far, it's proving to be enough."

"Enough of that bullshit! I can never and I will never forgive you for what you did. You didn't just steal my wife from me and also my daughter, but you also stole everything that meant something to me. I can never forgive you for destroying my life."

As soon as he finished saying that, he pointed his gun at me and I thought he was going to shoot me, but he was at a disadvantage. I already had my gun pointed at him and, thinking about my life, I pressed the trigger and the bullet came out of the barrel, hitting him in his head.

So that was it. After Gleb's fiasco, who was still in prison, the Punishers were no more.

But that was all beside the point right now. The most important thing was that I had my daughter with me, and she was still in the crib. She was crying, because of course she was. She was always crying, especially now after the shootout.

I grabbed her, holding her in my arms after tucking my gun under my pants.

She was the most precious thing in the world to me, and I just couldn't imagine myself living without her.

I turned around to see my men standing on the other side of the room, and I knew what that look on their faces was telling me. Even though we had gone through a lot, what just happened here would forever remain in our minds, and perhaps it would even lead to something else, even though I didn't think it was possible.

I was just happy that I had my daughter in my arms and that I was taking her out of this building now.

In the end, I didn't have the chance to tell Pavel that it wasn't his daughter. It was actually mine. When Barbara came with the news, I didn't know how to react.

But now, I could see that having my baby and building a family with her were everything I wanted, and nothing would ever change that.

It felt like everything had been resolved, but I knew that there were still some things that needed to be done.

After all, I just killed the entire Punishers MC and even though I didn't feel guilty about it, it still hurt me.

No matter, I thought. What mattered now was taking Ann back to Barbara, which I was already doing. I was going to ride back home safely and that was going to be the end of this.

CHAPTER 11

Barbara

That night, when he came back home, I knew that I should've done something so that he better appreciated being here with me. I should've made him his favorite food. It was dark and I knew that he hadn't eaten anything the entire day.

To be honest, I was just so overjoyed that he had come with Ann in his arms. I could see the blood on his face and on the rest of his body and clothes. He went through so much just for me, and that was a testament to his love for me.

I thought that everything was going to be okay since then. After all, he dealt with the problem, though that still left the police. Such carnage and the shootout. The police in New York City were looking for him. I didn't know if they would ever find out the whole truth, though.

Well, that was the life of the woman of a biker. His old lady. I didn't think that it would ever be different. It did make me feel concerned about the future, though.

It was a day after all of that happened, and I couldn't help but think how much I hated this place now.

The apartment, the city, and pretty much everything else.

I just couldn't see myself living here any longer now and soon we were going to be moving out. It couldn't be any different.

What I was thinking about faded as soon as my eyes found

my husband, who had just entered the bedroom after making sure that everything was okay with Ann. She was tucked under the covers in the crib and was sleeping like a rock.

It was a miracle, I thought. She was never like that unless she was dead tired.

Everything that happened was so fucked up that I would never tell her about it. She would always be kept in the dark about it all, for her own protection.

Igor was standing behind the door he just closed. I knew that look in his eyes and what it meant. He wanted to see me naked, didn't he? I asked myself. But there was no point in answering my own question, especially when I already knew the answer.

He put his fingers under his shirt and then he lifted it up, showing his perfect torso again. It was far from the first time I was seeing it, but there was still something special about it. There was always something special about him wanting to make love with me, and I knew I wanted it, too.

The moonlight entering the room shone just enough of his chest, making me wonder how much it was going to mean to me when my fingers were touching it.

I took a deep breath in.

I knew how much I wanted him now, and he was aware of that.

He took a step toward me and then another, and then one more, climbing onto the bed.

His body loomed in front of me.

I had to admit it. I didn't know what I was doing right now. I felt like a teenager all over again.

His hands started to feel me. Every part of me. My shoulders. My arms. My skin, and pretty much every other part of me that he could feel with his incessant fingers.

In the meantime, I just had to do the same. I felt his muscles and how hard they were. I felt their curves and I could tell that he thought he had just gone through the worst patch of his life.

Nothing could ever be compared to it.

His lips were so close to me now. I thought he was going to kiss me, but it was only a tease.

His fingers continued to feel me and he reached down, looking for my bundle of nerves.

My clit.

He started to rub it.

As soon as he entered the room, I had already started to strip myself naked. I prepared myself for this moment, for when his fingers were touching and monopolizing every part of me.

I could feel his breath on my face.

Even though he had gone through so much and suffered so much, it was like it didn't happen.

Everything was moving in slow motion and yet something wasn't. Me grabbing his dick. It was bigger than I remembered, even though not much time had passed since we last fucked.

I couldn't hold my gasp when it came out. I didn't even know why I reacted that way, given that this was far from the first time we were making love.

But it was different, wasn't it? I had really thought that he was going to die, but it didn't happen, and looking down, I couldn't help but feel some thirst in my mouth. My lips were dry.

I just had to reach down and put his cock into my mouth. It was so big and it stretched my lips beyond any level I thought possible. I never thought that he would be mine, that my ex-husband would be a non-factor in my life, and that I would ever have someone willing to help me so much and love me as much as Igor was.

My mind went back to my daughter, but she was happily sleeping in the crib, and I didn't think she would cry tonight. No fussing and waking up in the middle of the night. Still, I was certain that tonight I wasn't going to be getting much sleep.

My mind was such a whirlwind after everything that happened.

He kissed me once and then another time, his fingers moving over my breasts, feeling every part of them, and even pinching my nipples.

When he did that last thing, I arched my back. Just a normal reaction to feeling the immense pleasure that he showered me with.

"I don't know if I should be thinking about this and I don't even know if I should bring it up, but I think that it's about time we left this place for good. Our daughter is still an infant and we need to think about her future. I can find another job anywhere, and you know I'm right."

And I was. The only problem was that I was still kind of worried that the police were going to lock us up.

If they did that, I wouldn't be able to survive the following days. I couldn't help but worry that my daughter wouldn't be able to survive without me as well.

Nothing of that would ever happen, though.

His fingers brushed my lips, and I thought he was going to kiss me again, but he didn't.

I started to hump my body against him.

Feeling his massive dick against my pussy.

I wanted him inside of me.

When he fucked me that time in Las Vegas, he'd used a condom, but in the end, it didn't do anything, did it? He still knocked me up, and I couldn't help but wish for the same.

And he looked into my eyes, figuring out what I was thinking.

He was going to give me what I wanted.

He lowered his head so that it was between my legs. I'd seen that look in his eyes before, and I knew how rabid he was going to be right now.

He put his tongue out and started to lick and ravage my pussy with it, driving me crazy. I had no idea what was happening, but it was more than I thought it would ever be.

His fingers were all over me.

What was going on? I asked myself, feeling his fingers grazing my nipples.

This was so much more than I thought it would ever be.

Igor didn't stop when he started to flick his tongue over my pussy, and I knew that he was getting ready for his impending penetration.

And when that happened, it would be like everything I wanted from this moment.

He would knock me up, and I could just imagine that happening, his dick shooting another load in me, driving me wild.

I knew I was being slutty, but I wanted to be that way. I kept on rubbing my pussy against his prick, and I supposed that now was finally the time that we had been waiting to come this whole time.

He was going to penetrate me with his cock, and it was going to be painful and so rewarding at the same time. He didn't hold anything back, putting my legs over his shoulders and then finally penetrating me, one inch at a time.

It was just too much for me. I bit my bottom lip, and then he started a rhythm that he was comfortable with. He continued to pound in and out of my clenching sex, fucking me to oblivion, and I couldn't help but come at the same time as him, and it was exhilarating, my breathing accelerating.

I had really thought that he was going to reach for his condom, put it on, and finish this in a way that wouldn't be as satisfying.

But that wasn't what was happening, and that thought was good enough to open a huge grin on my face.

Igor then pulled out, plopping down on the bed by my side. He propped his head on his arm and looked at me, making me wonder what he was thinking.

And when he said what it was, I realized that I already knew it. "I love you."

And I couldn't help but tell him the same. I loved Igor just as much.

CHAPTER 12

Barbara

But not everything was going to be so perfect. When it came down to it, I was beginning to think that Igor just didn't want to move out.

I had no idea why, but one day he came up to me, saying over and over again that he just couldn't move out, even though we were beginning to think that the police were starting to figure out everything.

If they did, we would feel so paranoid about everything. His men were professional and he did make sure that he had set up everything so that they could never find out the truth, but that was the thing.

No matter how careful they had been about it, they could never and would never be so meticulous about it that it would be impossible for the police to know the truth.

I took a deep breath in.

I had taken a deep breath during that time.

I had thought that we had everything figured out, but the more I thought about what was really going on, the more I was beginning to realize that everything was so simple.

When it came down to it, Igor would never – and I meant that – stop being a biker. It was just in his nature, and there was nothing I could do about it.

That was why I was growing so frustrated about this issue.

The longer I continued to live in this place, the more I realized that it wasn't for me. I had really thought that I wanted to live in New York City, that it was going to be great to be among so many people, but now I realized that I had been fantasizing about it the wrong way, and I couldn't change that anymore.

The big, tall buildings.

The cold people.

The excessive lighting even though some streets were dark, a contrast that always scared me.

And also, how crowded everything was. Every place was crowded, and it was beginning to get on my nerves.

I had told Igor so many times about my issues with continuing to live here, but he just brushed it all off as though they were nothing to him. And that meant a lot to me.

It hurt me so much that I just couldn't keep living here, and I knew that meant I would soon make a decision I thought I would never pick in my life.

I had thought that everything was going to be like sunshine and rainbows, but I had not realized how much it meant to be living in a good place. A place where I didn't feel like the police were going to come after me all the time...

Not to mention that our baby was growing and I just couldn't give her enough attention while having to peek out the window every night, fearing that the police were going to knock on my door and then lock us in prison.

I couldn't help but wonder what would happen to my baby then. She would probably be put with another family and would be so confused that her mother wasn't with her anymore. I was certain that Igor would tell everyone that it was all only his fault and that I didn't have anything to do with it, but for me, it wasn't enough. His self-sacrifice wouldn't be enough.

What was even going on here? I didn't know, but it was confusing and I wanted it to end as soon as possible.

That was why I was probably doing the craziest thing of my life.

I was already leaving from here. I knew how he was going to

take it. He was going to start to think that I had someone else, but that really wasn't the case. It would never be. When it came down to it, I really loved Igor.

He hadn't come back from work yet. I knew that he was going to, but I was hoping that I was leaving the apartment much sooner and before that happened.

I just wanted to avoid the drama when it did happen.

My belly was growing bigger. When we had sex that time, I did want him to knock me up, and he did, but now it was making this harder than it should be. My body was so much bigger and heavier again.

But at least, I was getting out of this hellhole.

I had my bag in one hand and my baby in my other arm. Everyone that looked at me thought that something wrong was going on with me, but they never stopped to help me.

That was another issue I had with living here in New York City. The city was so big that nobody ever cared about anyone, and that was always so much so that it bothered me.

It made me wonder what it would be like if I was still living in Las Vegas, where the city was still relatively big, but at least there was a sense of community in the neighborhoods over there.

I took a deep breath, standing outside of the apartment building and hoping that my Uber was going to come here soon. I hoped so because the last thing I wanted was my husband stumbling on me out here, finding out that I was more than ready to abandon him.

The good thing was that his motorcycle was so loud and its noise was so distinct that I would hear it coming before it did. So far, I couldn't hear anything in the distance.

Everything was so dark.

I had no idea anymore how everything led to this moment.

I felt depressed and pissed off, and I just wanted it all to be different.

Would anyone ever hear my pleas?

I didn't know, but something good was happening. I knew that something good was about to turn everything for the better, and even though I had thought that hearing the engine of his motorcycle coming was going to destroy my strength, it did the opposite.

It made me feel more certain about this.

I'd thought that it would be my Uber pulling over, but this time it was my husband.

Igor was on his motorcycle, taking off his helmet.

His eyes were wide, but there was a sense of 'I knew this was going to happen one day' etched on his face. And as soon as he noticed how teary and red my eyes were, he jumped off the motorcycle and then threw his arms around me.

He put his hand on my chin and lifted my head so that I was looking into his eyes. And I was doing that with the utmost attention. I just wanted to know everything he was thinking and nothing, and no one would ever change that.

"I just want to leave this place as soon as possible. I don't know what you're thinking, trying to build another motorcycle club, but it's not going to work and it only makes me feel so much worse about this. I keep thinking that the police are going to knock on our door and that they are going to lock us up."

He took a deep breath, processing my words. After all, this was always going to be so difficult for him. He had been thinking that he could keep fooling the police, that he could start another motorcycle club and even call it The Punishers, but that would never be possible.

I was certain about that because I knew what he was going to say before he did.

"I know, love, but it still hurts me to see that you were willing to leave me without even saying anything about it. You were going to do the same thing that we did to Pavel, and it would have hurt me so much."

He wasn't someone to cry, but his eyes were slightly watery, and I could feel the strength with which he was holding me to his body. It wasn't enough to hurt me, but it was tight and I knew that he wouldn't open his arms without first assessing that everything was going to be okay with me.

He took a deep breath and then asked, "Is everything going to be okay now? Even though I don't like to think about it this way, but… you are right. We do need to leave New York City as soon as possible, and I'm thinking we should do that right now. Let's find a place that isn't America.

After all, if the police ever find out about what happened there, they would hunt us down throughout the entire country, and I just can't keep living and, at the same time, fearing that something like that might happen."

I kissed him. Of course he was going to do what I wanted. I was so ready to leave him, but now I could see that my husband had always been thinking about me only. The thing about him building another motorcycle club? It was nothing more than a pipe dream.

That was so clear to me now.

I supposed that, as a biker, he had always wanted to do that, even when he was with the Punishers, but now he knew differently and that the most important thing in his life was his family.

Me and the kids.

IGOR'S EPILOGUE

So, the Punishers were no more? Fat chance that happened, but I was keeping my hopes up about it. And also because the last thing I wanted was another motorcycle club coming after me. After all, there were so many of them that hated me so much.

They would always blame me for everything, wouldn't they?

But now we were living somewhere completely different. We were living in a country whose language we were still learning. Mexico. I never thought that I would come all the way down here to Mexico, but there was something charming about the country, and I was beginning to like it more and more.

I took a deep breath, standing just in front of the waves of the ocean. I was on the beach, and it couldn't be any different. I could feel the breeze around me. I could feel the sun on my face, and it wasn't hot.

It was actually pretty relaxing and slightly warm.

I took a deep breath in and I realized that my wife was by my side. She wasn't pregnant anymore. We had another baby, and this time it was a baby boy.

He was so cute and was sleeping in the crib. He was such a heavy sleeper, I thought, chuckling.

Differently from his sister, he liked to sleep a lot. Ann was a lot different. She liked to be more active, to be moving her arms around as much as she could, and to be crawling around on the floor until she was dead tired.

It was all great, but still... I couldn't help but feel that I had unresolved issues back in America.

I was certain that the remnants of the Punishers would pick up the pieces and rebuild the club from scratch. It was going to take time, and... Some rumors had come down here telling me about that. They didn't worry me, though.

I didn't think that they would ever come after me, and I was certain that this time they were finally going to choose a President that would always put the interests of the club above everything else.

It was what I was hoping for, anyway.

Her arm was around mine, linked with it. I looked down after I reopened my eyes and I found her face. I found her lips. I found her eyes and thought that the only thing I wanted to do right now was to kiss her.

That was what I was hoping for, but she was actually only teasing me. As soon as she realized that I was lowering my head, she started to move away from me. She started to the house on the beach that I built myself.

It took a lot of time, but in the end, I managed to build this house, and it was a lot better than I'd thought it would be.

Wouldn't you know it? I could actually be a good engineer when I wanted to. Could be promising, I hoped. Instead of focusing so much on being the best bodyguard possible, I could have a more respectable job.

Maybe I was a little old for it, but that was what I was thinking about right now.

It just wasn't an issue.

I went after her inside the house, assaulted by the familiarity of the place. We had been living here long enough to know everything about it. Every nook and cranny.

And then, I was somewhere that made me feel even better.

I was in the room that I'd built for my babies. Ann was a little bigger now, so she couldn't sleep in the crib anymore. She had her own bed. It was small, but the pillow and the mattress were soft as though they were made of feathers.

"What do you want to show me, my love?" I asked, noticing

that my wife had something she was holding behind her with her hands. I didn't know what it was, but I was so curious about it that I was almost even reaching behind her with my hand.

I even tried to do that, but she avoided my attempt, and now I knew that I had to be a little bit more patient about it so that I didn't ruin the surprise.

"It's just something that I thought it's going to make you forget everything bad that happened before coming here."

She was holding the box in her hand, and it was small. Something that was going to make me forget everything that happened before coming to Mexico? I didn't know why she was telling me that, but either way, I didn't think it was possible.

Still, I couldn't help but open the box anyway.

And when I lifted the lid, I knew she was right about the gift she was giving to me.

BARBARA'S EPILOGUE

I honestly didn't think that I would ever make a friend here in Mexico. Well, maybe I should have thought that eventually someone was going to mix well with me, and it was so great that that person was none other than the woman that was sitting on the couch, by my side.

"I can't believe that you married a biker," she said to me, smiling broadly. She put down the glass that she was holding in her hand. We were drinking together. We were doing that and shooting the breeze, and getting to know each other, too.

She was my friend, but there was so much about her that I needed to know.

It wasn't that I needed to know everything about her, but that I wanted her to have the best.

I knew that I had something now I'd thought I never would. I was married, had two kids, and a good husband that loved me. He was precious, and so was everyone that was still part of my life.

As for my mother, she was better now. She was still in the hospital, but she was doing better and she had even woken up, too. I couldn't be happier about that.

The police hadn't come for us yet, and I didn't think that they would anytime soon. It looked like the search for what had happened in the apartment building was still ongoing and it had hit a low point recently, with not much progress happening.

When Igor said that he had been meticulous about the carnage when it happened, he didn't lie to me, and the more the years passed, the more I began to think that nothing would ever come out of that… Incident.

Of course, Amelia would never learn the truth. I could never and I would never tell her anything about the things that my husband did when he was with the Punishers.

I was so over all that, anyway.

"Yes, and I'm so happy that we are together. We went through so much."

Igor was working now and recently he had gotten a job in an engineering company. Building buildings. The more I thought about it, the more I loved it, and the more I felt that he really was the right man for me.

As soon as he realized that he should never and couldn't continue being a biker, and thinking that he was going to start another motorcycle club, was the moment when he made the best decision of his life.

He decided that we should be together and live here in Mexico.

We were living far from the border with the United States as well. I just couldn't imagine living near there and fearing that the police could cross the border and then lock us up.

At least, if they ever started that, we would have enough time to know about it before it was too late.

Amelia and I had been talking, and we continued our little chit-chat until we could see the sun setting in the distance.

When we realized that it was already so late that her family was going to be worried about her if she didn't leave right now, she stood up and I led her to the door out of the house.

I opened it for her and said, "I know that you're going through a lot and I can kind of see myself in you, but everything is going to be fine. For what it's worth, what happened to me… I know that you think it might never happen to you, but you might be surprised. You might find love somewhere where you think there isn't any."

She was smiling. Such a shy, innocent smile. Well, there were bikers in Mexico as well. Amelia could get lucky.

She was always smiling, and it was something about her that I loved. Perhaps it was the fact that we were in Mexico and here the people were happier, but if that was really the case, I didn't know for sure.

Either way, I would never mention something like that because I knew it would be weird.

"Well, I'm sure as hell hoping that I'm going to find someone as sexy as your husband," she joked and I smiled too, chuckling. Even though it was the first time that she ever said something about my husband's looks, it didn't rattle me.

I knew that my husband was hot, and I was also so certain that he would never cheat on me.

His love for me was so deep that the thought would never even cross his mind.

"I'm sure you're going to find someone that's going to make you happy, but I'm certain that he won't be as sexy as Igor," I said, content that she was happy and still smiling even as she left.

She entered her car and then rode off to her house, making me wonder what was going to happen to her.

In the meantime, I just noticed that Igor was coming here in his car. He had bought that sedan after he realized that he had gotten tired of motorcycles.

And seeing that, I opened another huge grin.

It was so great to know that I would always have my husband coming home for me and the kids.

The End

Thank you and leave your review. Your feedback helps me immensely.

TEASER: BIKER'S REJECTED BABY

Dark Mafia MC Romance

"The only thing you're good for is having my baby," my husband barked, shoving me backward with his hand. He was strong enough to do that, and I felt myself colliding against the wall. He was huffing in front of me, behaving as though he was going to hurt me more than he already did.

Lifting my head up slowly, I looked at him and I couldn't see the person that I once fell in love with. He was so much different now. Or maybe I was stupid when I fell in love with him. I even married him. The ring that was on my finger was a constant reminder of that.

It was a reminder of something I could never, ever change, unless I wanted to put my life at risk.

The stench that was coming out of his mouth... It showed me that he was drinking a lot before coming back home. He was always like that. I didn't know if it was because of me, but Gleb always drank so much. He always got so drunk that he started to become violent toward me, just like now.

Not to mention that I was sure he was seeing someone behind my back. The hickey on his neck told me as much, and he wasn't even ashamed of it. If he was, he would have tried to hide it, but the smear of the lipstick on his skin was so clear that he didn't even try to rub it off with his hand.

He wasn't cornering me, but our bedroom was small enough to make me feel as though it could only fit the two of us in it.

"I'm not going to give you a baby. Never!" I shouted, making my point clear. The only comforting thing about this was that he was beyond raping someone to have his baby. I wasn't saying that that would never change, but the thought comforted me, for now. At least for now I could rely on the fact that he wasn't going to do something like that.

I supposed that was something good thanks to the fact that he was seeing someone else – at least he was sating his sex urges with her. I wondered who she was, I thought before lifting myself up a little more so that I didn't look so submissive in front of him.

Gleb was the president of The Punishers MC, one of the most feared and respected biker gangs in the country. His name carried a certain weight that put most men below him. Most men here in Las Vegas feared him, and I was certain that was something that would never change.

And even though he always struck fear in my heart, I wasn't going to show that I was afraid of him. If I did something like that, he wouldn't hesitate before doing something to me that even he would regret.

"Is that so?" He said, his voice low and threatening. He approached me and then put his hand on my chin again. This time, he was much gentler about it. He wasn't digging his fingers into my skin, something that I found myself thankful about. "Do you know what that means, Isabel?"

I was staring back at his eyes. If he was thinking that he was going to make me submit to his wishes simply by looking at me with threatening eyes, then he was going to be disappointed.

After living for so many years with a drunkard for a husband, I was courageous enough to stand up for myself, even if only a little.

I nodded once and slowly, even though he was pushing my head up with his hand. "Yeah, I'm certain about that. You aren't going to change my mind about it."

"You are such a bitch," he said before fisting his other hand and then punching the wall behind me. I had no idea if he hurt himself doing that, but he had to have. After all, the punch was so loud that I felt as though he just hit me instead. Not to mention that I also felt the wall trembling slightly.

I knew that Gleb was strong, but I never thought his strength was so unparalleled. I doubted there was anyone that could match him in terms of physical strength.

He was still staring back at me, into my eyes, and I could feel as though his eyes were burning with hatred for me. When I married him, he was so much kinder and more relatable. He even said how much he loved me, and it had to have been a lie.

It had to be. Nothing more than a hateful lie.

He retreated his hand and I noticed that it was smeared with red marks and little pieces of the wallpaper. He didn't seem to mind that, though, which was probably because he wasn't even aware of it. He was so drunk that he couldn't even feel the pain that I was sure he would be feeling otherwise.

And then his other hand fell to the side of his body. He was still huffing slightly, but after his display of strength, it was obvious that he was beginning to calm down a little, something I was thankful for.

A moment of silence fell into the room, and I wondered if he was going to do something else. After all, he had just turned around so that his back was facing me.

Even though now he was finally a couple of steps away from me, he still looked so massive it was frightening.

I was strong. At least, I was doing everything to show that I wasn't completely, utterly terrified of him. If I wasn't, I would probably have crumbled and fallen to the floor.

My legs were weak, but I was holding on to whatever strength I still had to keep myself up.

Minutes later, he finally muttered something, and then I wondered what he was going to do. Without telling me anything else, Gleb walked out of the room, and his gait was slow and his back was slightly hunched. I had no idea if he felt some shame –

finally – over what he did, but I didn't care about that.

I opened my mouth and I let out a huge cloud of my breath that I was holding in my lungs. Now that my husband wasn't in our room anymore after storming inside it shouting that he wanted his baby, I could finally calm down.

So, I dragged myself over to the bed and then I sat down on it slowly. My hand was shaking, but I was holding up as much as I could.

I lifted my head up, looking around the room. There wasn't anything special about it. Even though Gleb was the president of The Punishers MC, he wasn't particularly rich.

It wasn't for his wealth that I married him, after all. I just fell in love with him, as I said before.

He was everything to me back then.

A bed, a closet, some decorative items, the logo of The Punishers MC hanging from the wall opposite me, and hints that he was smoking marijuana the day before, and I remembered that there wasn't anything special about this room. He always smoked that drug and I hated it. I couldn't even stand the smell.

Minutes later, when I felt that I was finally feeling better, I stood up and padded over to the bathroom. I took off my clothes, turned on the shower head, and then let the water wash away my festering thoughts.

The water and the steam coming from it were enough to make me feel better and think straight. If there was something that I learned while living here and with Gleb, it was that I couldn't make decisions in the heat of the moment, and now was one of those times.

Minutes later, I finished my shower. I turned off the shower head, walked out of the shower box, and then put on a fresh set of clothes that had been washed the other day. Nothing like wearing new clothes with that smell of lavender after taking a hot shower to feel better, especially after a tumultuous moment like the one that just happened with Gleb.

Not much was happening around here. We lived in the suburbs. There wasn't much of value in the house, but at least the neighborhood was quiet most of the time. I could even hear Gleb in the living room, probably watching TV and drinking some more, even after drinking as much as he could in that pub downtown.

Just thinking about it, I felt my stomach churning. There were few things in the world worse than that pub. That's where most of his gang members assembled, especially when they had something important to discuss, like the next store they were going to hit after not paying for their protection.

Las Vegas was falling more and more into the world of corruption, decay, crimes, and the like. Reflecting on that, I couldn't help but think that soon it was going to be so ridden with those things that I would have to move out.

Hell, moving out was something that I should be doing right at this moment...

ABOUT THE AUTHOR

Gabrielle Melo writes steamy dark romances. Her stories are peppered with mafia bosses, MC bikers, and gripping and intense scenes. Love conquers all is her motto. It doesn't matter what challenges her characters face – her books always end with their HEAs.